T0398510

BAREFOOT SKATEBOARDERS

Rina Singh

illustrated by
Sophie Casson

ORCA BOOK PUBLISHERS

Hidden in the heart of India lies Janwaar, a remote village. A single unfinished road runs through it. On one side live the Yadavs, who own farmland and have brick homes. On the other side are Adivasis, Indigenous people who work as farm laborers and have mud houses.

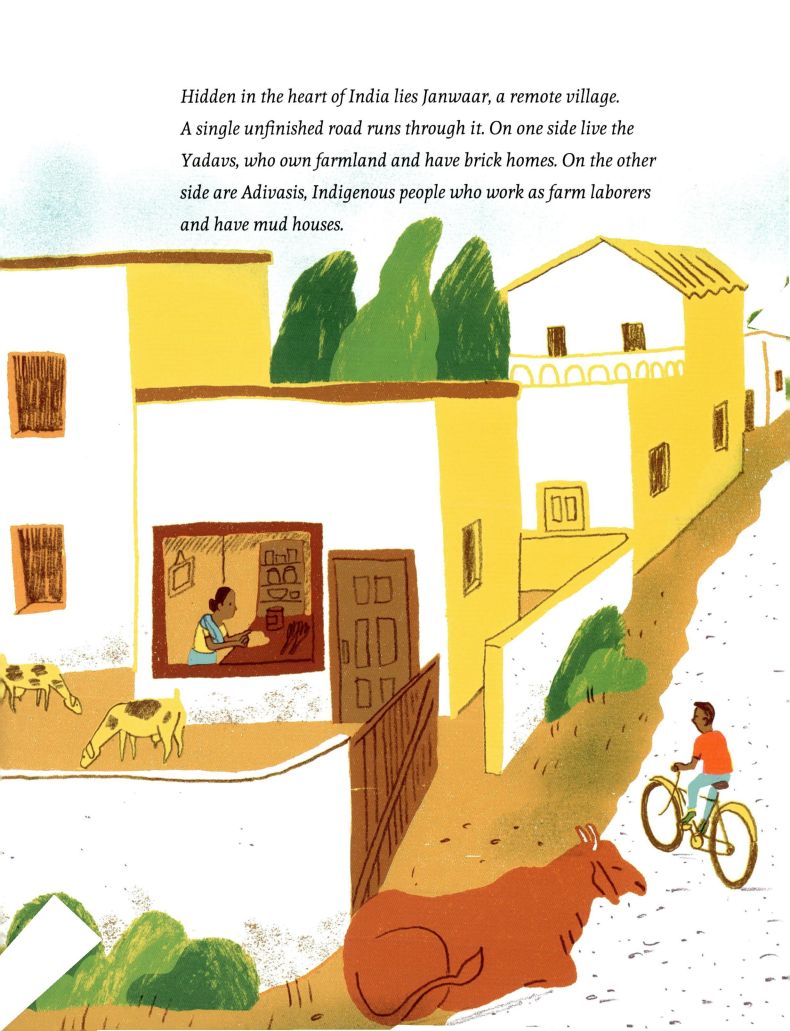

At the school, Yadavs don't allow their children to play or eat with Adivasis. At the well, Yadav women draw the water first. That's how it has always been. Yadavs never let Adivasis forget their place in the world.

Janwaar is a tiny village, but it's not a quiet one. There's a big construction project underway, and Ramkesh has come to watch. He sees many workers busy at the site.

What are they building? Another school? A hospital?

With pointless hills and ramps, the structure looks like a waste of concrete!

When the construction is done, Ramkesh checks it out from nearby. For three days he watches a small group of boys playing on its slopes, gliding on strange boards with wheels.

The foreigner who always seems to be there sees him and calls him over.

He hesitates. "Adivasi." He points at himself.
"Ulrike." She points at herself.
Hmm. The fact that he's an Adivasi doesn't
matter to her. He shrugs and smiles.

Ulrike offers Ramkesh a wooden board with four wheels.

"Skateboard," she says.

He realizes this new place is for everyone, even Adivasis.

Ramkesh isn't sure what to do at first.

Ulrike shows him videos of kids riding their skateboards and taking off into the air.

The first thing he notices is their shoes.

Flashy. Bright. Beautiful.

Ramkesh looks down at his dusty bare feet and jumps on the board. He tries to balance and copy their moves.

He falls, scrapes his knees and falls again.

But every time, he picks himself up.

He wants to fly too.

Soon the rest of the boys join him, and the skate park becomes their new playground.

The parents aren't sure what to do. Yadav and Adivasi children have never played together. They worry there will be fights. But they decide to watch and wait.

At the skate park, no one brings up Yadav. No one mentions Adivasi.

The divide begins to blur.

But where are the girls?

Ramkesh asks his sister Durgha to come to the park. She is excited to join.

Soon other girls come too. When they are too shy to approach the boys, a rule goes up.

Girls First

Any girl can say "Girls first" to a boy
and get a turn at the board.

The village begins to fill with the laughter and shrieks of barefoot children and the clickety-clack of the skateboards. Ramkesh is getting really good.

It's so much fun that some children start skipping school to be at the park. And a new rule goes up.

No School, No Skateboarding

Word spreads. Soon journalists, photographers and filmmakers flock to Janwaar.

Famous skateboarders from Brazil, Canada and the United States hear the buzz too. They travel all the way to India to be part of the children's adventure. They make videos of the kids, who show off for the cameras, and share them with the world.

And, even better, they teach the kids new tricks.
Grinds. Ollies. Backflips. Kickflips. Powerslides.
The children feel free when they are on their
skateboards. Like Ramkesh, they all want wings to fly.

Curious and smart, Ramkesh becomes a champion skateboarder in the village. Even the older boys look up to him.

Thanks to their talent, Ramkesh
and his neighbors, Asha and Arun,
are invited to travel. They are the first
children in the village to get passports.
And they're all Adivasis.

Ramkesh and Arun are going to Germany. Asha is heading
to London. None of them has ever seen an airplane before.
Ramkesh looks at his new shoes.
It is a big moment.

The boys fall in love with Berlin, where they get to try out different skate parks (and ice cream!). They go to other cities too. Antwerp. Paris. Bordeaux. Barcelona. It's a whirlwind of a tour.

They watch in awe as skateboarders shred huge skate parks with ease.

In Janwaar they thought they were champions. Now they realize they have a lot to learn.

The children come back home humbled but energized, and with new dreams—for themselves and for the village.

Ramkesh, Asha and Arun bring the villagers together with their newfound confidence. Everyone is proud that the world knows about Janwaar. For the first time in their lives, the elders let their children lead the way.

Today the road through Janwaar is still unfinished. But a change has come over its people. They have hope in their smiles. A purpose in their eyes—to support each other, to keep learning.

And the village is filled with the laughter and shrieks of barefoot children and the clickety-clack of their skateboards.

They are beginning to find their place in the world.

The author with some of the Janwaar skateboarders.

Author's Note

In 2018 I spent four glorious days in Janwaar and watched the little barefoot skateboarders ripping up the skate park. Earlier that year I had met Ulrike Reinhard, a German activist, in Delhi. Inspired by the success of the skate park Skateistan in Afghanistan, she started Janwaar Castle in this rural village in Madhya Pradesh, India.

In 2014 she asked fifteen artists worldwide, including Ai Weiwei, to transform skateboards into artboards. The boards were auctioned as a fundraiser, and she built the skate park with the proceeds. Twelve skateboarders from six different countries, including multiple world champion Nyjah Huston from California, volunteered to design and construct the park with the locals. An incredible story of social, cultural and economic change unfolded. Ulrike did not coach the children, because she's not a skateboarder. Instead children are the driving force. Empowered by the skills of skateboarding, they became the actual changemakers.

Ramkesh with his mother.

I was so excited to hear about what was happening in Janwaar that I planned to see it for myself. I returned to India later in the year, took an overnight train from Delhi to Khajuraho and then a taxi to Janwaar. After touring the village and seeing the kids' brilliant skateboarding skills in action, I visited their homes and talked to their mothers. Ramkesh's mother unwrapped a piece of cloth and proudly showed me her son's passport. He beamed as his mother spoke of his achievements as a skateboarder. Skateboarding has given the villagers identity.

I left Janwaar with my heart full and promised to stay in touch. For a year I volunteered and taught some of the children English via Skype. It used to be the highlight of my Sunday mornings. I'm still available for them when they need help.

So, it is with great joy that I bring the story of the barefoot skateboarders to young readers.

For Maninder and Ulrike, who made it possible.
—R.S.

To your inner strength, reader.
— S.C.

Published in Canada and the United States in 2024 by Orca Book Publishers.
orcabook.com

Library and Archives Canada Cataloguing in Publication
Title: Barefoot skateboarders / Rina Singh ; illustrated by Sophie Casson.
Names: Singh, Rina, 1955– author. | Casson, Sophie, illustrator.
Identifiers: Canadiana (print) 20230553087 | Canadiana (ebook) 20230553095 |
ISBN 9781459838536 (hardcover) | ISBN 9781459838543 (PDF) | ISBN 9781459838550 (EPUB)
Subjects: LCSH: Skateboarding—India—Madhya Pradesh—Juvenile literature. | LCSH: Children—India—Madhya Pradesh—Juvenile literature. | LCSH: Social change—India—Madhya Pradesh—Juvenile literature. | LCGFT: Picture books.
Classification: LCC GV859.8 .S56 2024 | DDC j796.220954/3—dc23

Library of Congress Control Number: 2023947594

Summary: In this nonfiction picture book, the tiny village of Janwaar in Madhya Pradesh, India, gets a new skatepark, which inspires Ramkesh and all the local kids to learn how to skateboard, putting them on the map and uniting their community.

Orca Book Publishers is committed to reducing the consumption of nonrenewable resources in the production of our books. We make every effort to use materials that support a sustainable future.

Orca Book Publishers gratefully acknowledges the support for its publishing programs provided by the following agencies: the Government of Canada, the Canada Council for the Arts and the Province of British Columbia through the BC Arts Council and the Book Publishing Tax Credit.

Artwork created using hand-drawn pencil illustrations that are scanned, digitally colored and finished with a textured overlay, such as handmade stamps or stencilling with dry pastels or oil pencil.

Cover and interior artwork by Sophie Casson
Design by Rachel Page
Edited by Sarah Howden

Printed and bound in South Korea.

27 26 25 24 • 1 2 3 4

Rina Singh is an award-winning children's author who is drawn to real-life stories about the environment and social justice. Her critically acclaimed and award-winning books include *Grandmother School*, winner of the 2021 Christie Harris Illustrated Children's Literature Prize; *Diwali: A Festival of Lights*, nominated for the Red Cedar Award; and *Once, a Bird*. Rina has an MFA in creative writing from Concordia University and a teaching degree from McGill University. She lives in Toronto.

Sophie Casson has illustrated more than 25 books, including *The Artist and Me* by Shane Peacock, a finalist for the Marilyn Baillie Picture Book Award, and *Helen's Birds* by Sara Cassidy, selected as part of IBBY Canada's Silent Book collection. Her highly acclaimed illustrations are inspired by etchings, silkscreen works and Japanese woodblock prints. Sophie's award-winning work has also appeared in the *Globe and Mail*, the *New York Times*, the *Financial Times*, the *Los Angeles Times* and *Nature*, as well as in the Canadian Museum for Human Rights. Sophie lives in Montreal.